SNOW WHITE

RETOLD BY JOSEPHINE POOLE

AND ILLUSTRATED BY
ANGELA BARRETT

ALFRED A. KNOPF · NEW YORK

ONCE UPON A TIME, THERE WAS A CA??? in a wild place. A king and queen lived ??? there; they loved each other dearly, and were happy.

One day the queen sat by the window, stitching pearls onto cloth of gold. It was winter and very cold, and presently it began to snow.

She opened the window to listen for the sound of the king's hunting horn. But as she leaned out, she pricked herself with her needle, so that a drop of blood fell onto the snow. When she saw it, she wished in her heart, "Oh, that I had a child as red as blood, as white as snow, and as black as the wood of an ebony tree!"

And her wish came true, for in the course of time she had a daughter, the most beautiful baby girl that ever was seen. She was called Snow White, for her skin was white as snow; also her lips were red as blood, and her hair as black as ebony. But, alas! The poor young queen died when she was born.

the king was distracted with grief and would have shut himself up in his wild kingdom, but — for the child's sake — after a year he married again. His new bride was very young, and very beautiful; everybody said she was the most beautiful lady in the whole world. Nobody told him that she had a proud heart and a greedy, jealous temper. Nobody mentioned that.

Now, this queen had a magic mirror, which hung on her bedroom wall. Sometimes, when she was alone, she would unveil it and look at herself — this way, that way — and oh! she was superlatively beautiful. After that she would whisper into the glass, sweetly, pleasantly,

> "Mirror, mirror on the wall,
>
> Who is the fairest of us all?"

And a soft, magical voice always answered,

> "You are the fairest of them all."

Then the proud queen was satisfied.

Snow White lived in a different part of the castle. She had her nurse and her own cook. When she was old enough, a governess came to instruct her, and an old gentleman to teach her music and dancing. Years passed, and she grew to be so kind, and gentle, and funny, and clever, that everybody loved her.

Only the king did not visit her as often as he should, because she reminded him too painfully of the dead queen, her mother, whom he still loved. As for her stepmother, she thought Snow White a timid, poor-spirited child, not worth a second glance.

But one day, when the stepmother queen bent her beautiful head to the magic looking glass, and asked as usual:

"Mirror, mirror on the wall,
Who is the fairest of us all?"

the mirror answered:

"Queen, you are full fair, 'tis true,
But Snow White fairer is than you."

Then the queen was horribly shocked. Her beautiful face turned yellow with envy and rage, and from that moment she hated Snow White with all her heart. She could get no different answer out of the mirror, and she knew that it spoke the truth.

The queen's wicked passions grew in her, until she had no peace, day or night. At last she sent for a certain huntsman who was discontented with the king's service. She said to him, "You must take that evil girl Snow White into the forest and kill her, and bring me back her heart as proof."

He looked at her and said, "What will you give me if I do it?"

So she handed him a purse full of gold.

Next day, when Snow White went riding, the huntsman lay in wait for her, and he grabbed her pony by the bridle, and led her deep into the forest by secret paths no one could follow. Then he pulled out his knife. But the trembling maiden threw herself at his feet, weeping and pleading for mercy. And she was so lovely, and cried so piteously, that in the end he could not bear to hurt her; besides, he knew that wild beasts would devour her quickly enough once night fell. He killed a young boar instead and cut out its heart, which he gave secretly to the queen as a token.

The king sent all his soldiers into the forest to look for Snow White, but she was nowhere to be found. So everyone went into mourning for her, and many bitter tears were shed. Even the wicked queen dressed herself in black velvet, while she was exulting in her heart.

Now when the huntsman rode away, leaving Snow White alone in the forest, she stared about her in terror; even the rustling of the trees made her heart beat pit-a-pat. So she started to run. And the wild beasts of the forest ran too, but for company, not to harm her; they pitied her as she fled, bruising her poor feet and scratching herself on the brambles that grew everywhere under the trees.

She ran on and on until she was utterly exhausted. She had reached a clearing in the forest; it was already evening, and one star shone in the patch of sky above the trees. There in front of her stood a little house, with a neat garden all round. She went up the path and knocked on the door. Nobody answered.... Still nobody.... But she was so tired that she could not help it, she had to go in to rest.

The door opened into a nice clean kitchen. There was a table spread with a cloth and laid for supper: seven little plates of bread and cheese she counted, and seven little cups of wine. She was so hungry and thirsty that she took just a mouthful of bread and cheese from each plate, so as not to finish a helping. From each cup she took a sip of wine.

In the next room she found seven little beds lined against the wall, each with a spotless white pillow and quilt. She was so tired that she lay down on one of them, and praying to God that He would look after her, she fell asleep.

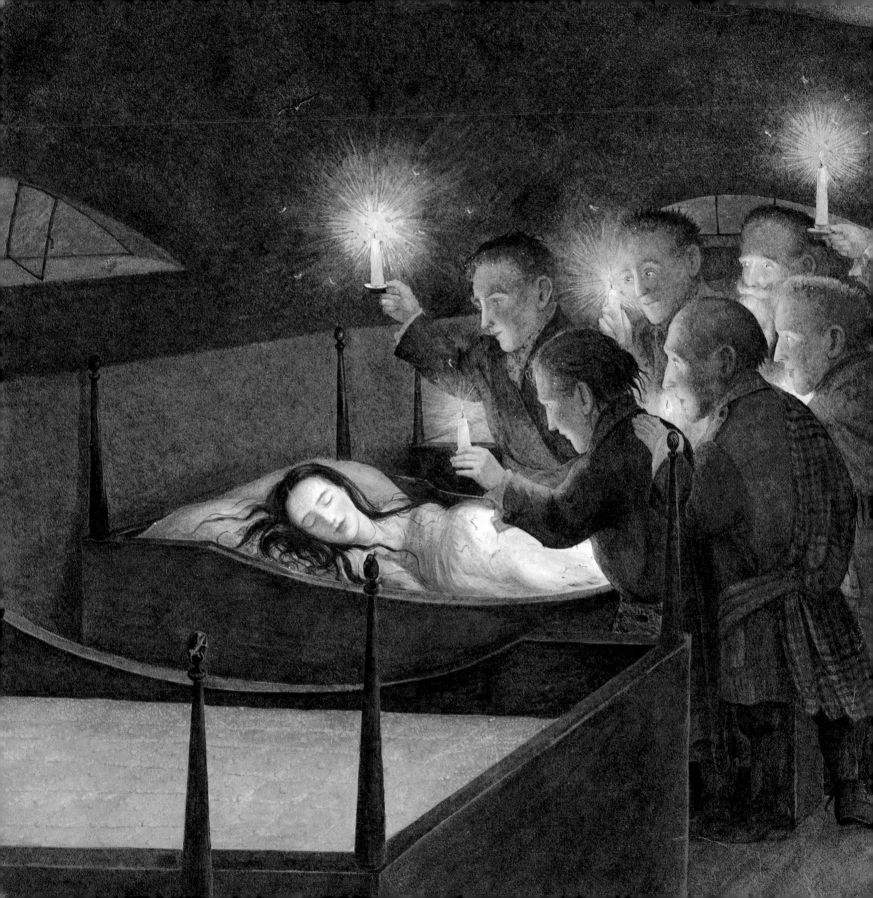

Now, this little house belonged to a family of dwarfs, who toiled all day in the gold mines, deep within the mountains.

When it was quite dark, they came home, and they noticed at once that somebody had called while they were out. So they struck flint and lit their seven candles, so that the room was a blaze of light.

First they saw that their suppers had been tasted, and next they found Snow White, fast asleep in the little white bed. They crowded round her, lifting up their candles with cries of astonishment. "Oh goodness! Oh gracious!" they exclaimed. "What beautiful child is this?" And they were full of joy and excitement, though they were careful not to wake her.

Snow White was very frightened next morning when she went into the kitchen and saw seven little men sitting round the table. But they were polite and friendly, and when she had told them her story, they said, "If you will keep house for us, cook and clean and wash and sew and knit, you may stay with us, and we will look after you always."

"With all my heart," said Snow White, and so the bargain was made. All day the seven dwarfs were away digging for gold in the mountain. When they came home, they found their supper ready, their clothes clean and mended, and the house neat as a new pin. So the weeks passed. But the good dwarfs never forgot to warn Snow White as they left the house each morning. "Beware of your stepmother, the wicked queen!" they said. "She will soon find you out. Take care, do not let anybody in!"

Now, the queen was sure that Snow White was dead. But one day she drew back the veil from the magic looking glass.

"Mirror, mirror on the wall,

Who is the fairest of us all?"

she asked with a smile. To her astonishment, the soft voice replied,

"O Queen, thou art of beauty rare,

But Snow White, living in the glen

With the seven little men,

Is a thousand times more fair."

The queen turned white with fury, and her eyes glinted like a serpent's. She never doubted the mirror; she knew at once that the huntsman had deceived her, but he had gone where she could not get at him. So she disguised herself as an ugly old woman, and set off secretly to the house of the seven dwarfs.

The queen could not find her way through the forest; besides, the wild beasts would certainly have eaten her. So, instead, she had to walk a long and weary way, over seven mountains, until at last she came to the cottage. She limped up the path crying, "Collars and laces, belts and buttons! Pretty trifles for wives and maidens!"

Snow White called from the window, "Good day, Granny. What have you to sell?"

Then the old woman held up the silken laces, which so pleased Snow White that she said to herself, What harm can there be in this good old woman? So she unbarred the door, and the peddler woman glided in.

"What a beautiful figure you have, my dear, to be sure!" she exclaimed. This was true, though she only pretended to admire it. "You shall have the laces as a present, only let me thread them for you."

And with quick fingers she threaded the colored silks into Snow White's bodice, in and out, all the way up. Then she pulled them so tight that the poor girl could not breathe and fell senseless to the ground. "So much for the fairest!" screeched the wicked queen, and she scuttled away in her old-woman's shawl, like a spider.

The seven dwarfs, when they returned, were horrified to find Snow White lying as dead on the floor. However, they noticed how tightly she was laced, and they cut the bright silk at once, so that little by little she came back to life. Then she told them what had happened, and they cried out, "O dear child, you cannot see evil in anyone! The wicked queen has been here. You must be more careful, you must not let anybody in!"

As soon as the queen reached the castle, she hurried to her magic mirror and demanded with a beating heart,

"Mirror, mirror on the wall,
Who is the fairest of us all?"

But the glass replied,

"O Queen, thou art of beauty rare,
But Snow White, living in the glen
With the seven little men,
Is a thousand times more fair."

Then she knew her plan had failed, and her face became dark and hideous, reflecting the passions in her heart.

The queen had a little room, at the top of an empty tower, full of bats and spiders. Here she schemed, and poured, and scraped, and stirred, until she had brewed something very poisonous in her cauldron. Then she fetched a jeweled comb and steeped it in the brew, and when it was ready, she wrapped it carefully in a cloth. She disguised herself once more, and set out for the cottage of the seven dwarfs. It was a long, long way over the seven mountains, but her envious heart drove her on.

When Snow White heard her at the door, she looked out of the window.

"You must go away," she said. "I cannot let anybody in." But the evil woman held up the comb, so that the jewels in it caught the light most enticingly. Then she exclaimed, "Why, what beautiful hair you have! If you have been forbidden to let anybody in, then you must not. Only lean out of the window, and let me comb your beautiful hair."

Snow White leaned out of the window, so that her black hair hung down like a curtain of silk. But no sooner did the comb touch it, than its poison was released. The girl gave one cry and fainted dead away.

The poor little dwarfs were in a terrible fright when they discovered their beloved Snow White, and, indeed, she would have died, only they came home earlier than expected. They soon found the comb and pulled it out of her hair, and then gradually the color came back into her cheeks, and she opened her eyes. "O sweet child," they said, as they rubbed her cold hands and sponged her face with wine and water, "you must be always on your guard. Your stepmother is evil and cunning, and she will stop at nothing to destroy you!"

Far away, the queen stood in front of her magic mirror.

"Mirror, mirror on the wall,

Who is the fairest of us all?"

But once more it answered,

"O Queen, thou art of beauty rare,

But Snow White, living in the glen

With the seven little men,

Is a thousand times more fair."

The queen was now so furious that she wanted to smash the glass with her clenched fists. Instead, she crept up to her secret room, and she toiled there many days. And at last she had prepared a poisonous apple, so deadly that she herself was almost afraid of it. She hid it in a basket of fruit, and herself in a third disguise. So she set off across the seven mountains, and that was a long, long way; but she sped on her wicked feet and by and by arrived at the cottage.

Snow White heard the click of the gate and looked out. She could not see that this sunburned peasant woman was the silver-haired granny with the laces and the peddler with the poisoned comb. She called out, "I am sorry, but I cannot let you in. The seven dwarfs have forbidden me to open the door!" Still, she looked longingly at the fruit, all ripe and delicious in the woman's basket.

"Never mind, you are wise to be careful, and I shall take my fruit somewhere else. Bless you, pretty face! I shall leave you an apple, all the same," and she pretended to select the finest, and showed it to Snow White, who shook her head at the window.

"Indeed, I cannot take it. I promised them I would not!"

"Are you afraid of poison? But I shall cut it, and eat half myself."

For the apple was made so that all the poison was in the red side. "The white for me, and you shall have the red!" cried the old woman, and took a bite from the white half and handed the rosy piece to Snow White, who then could not resist biting into it. As soon as she tasted it, she shrieked and fell as if she had been stabbed in the heart. Then the wicked queen leered at her through the window, and cackled like a witch, "Well, well, my dear! I think you have done with being the fairest!"

As soon as she got home, the queen hastened to unveil her looking glass.

> "Mirror, mirror, on the wall,
> Who is the fairest of us all?"

Then at last came the reply,

> "You are fairest now of all."

So at last her jealous heart had peace — as much as a jealous heart can have.

The good little dwarfs came home at sunset. Once more they found their beloved Snow White lying as dead upon the ground, but this time nothing they did could bring her back to life. They unlaced her, combed out her hair, washed her with water and wine — it was no use. Then they were full of grief, and prayed and lamented three bitter days, clustered round her bed in tears. After that, they would have buried her, except that they could not bear to put her into the ground; for her cheeks were still pink, as if she was sleeping and not dead.

So they made a glass coffin, and laid her in it, and wrote on it in letters of gold, "I am Snow White, a king's daughter." Then they carried out the coffin, and arranged a place for it on the mountainside, and took it in turns so that one of them always watched over it. Three birds also came there to mourn for Snow White — an owl, a raven, and a dove.

Snow White lay in her glass coffin on the mountainside, and the days passed, the weeks and months passed, but she never changed — she was still as white as snow, as red as blood, and as black as ebony.

One day, it chanced that a prince rode that way who had been hunting in the forest. And when he looked in the coffin and saw Snow White, he fell straightway in love with her. He gazed at her long and long, and at last he said to the dwarfs, "Let me have the coffin, and I will give you whatever you ask."

The dwarfs told him that they could not part with it for all the money in the world. But he begged more and more. "Dear dwarfs," he said, "I cannot live without this maiden. I beseech you to give her to me. I swear I shall honor you always, and look after you as if you were my brothers."

So at last they pitied him, and allowed him to take the coffin, and the prince told his servants to carry it away on their shoulders. But as they were taking it down the mountain, one of them stumbled, and the crumb of poison flew out of Snow White's throat. She stirred, opened her eyes, and astonished at finding herself in a glass box, raised the lid and sat up, alive and well. Then the prince and the dwarfs were overcome with joy at the miracle, and the prince, falling at once to his knees, begged the beautiful girl to be his bride.

He took her to his father's castle, and the seven dwar[f] made his counselors. A splendid feast was arranged, an[d] wedding invitations were sent out all through the coun[try.] The stepmother queen received one; she did not know [who] the bride was. She put on her grandest clothes, and stoo[d] front of her magic looking glass for the last time, and sa[id,]

> "Mirror, mirror on the wall,
>
> Who is the fairest of us all?"

But the soft voice answered,

> "O Queen, although you are of beauty rare,
>
> The young bride is a thousand times more fair."

The queen then raged and swore, and bit her nails a[nd] vowed she would not go to the wedding. However, she [had to] go, because there could be no peace for her until she sa[w the] bride. But she took with her a poisonous rose, which sh[e] meant to leave on the young bride's pillow.

When she saw that it was Snow White who was marr[ied,] so happy and so beloved, the evil queen turned quite m[ad] with jealousy, so that in her passion she clutched the de[adly] rose. Then she died miserably of her own poison.

But Snow White and her prince, and the seven vene[rable] counselors, lived happily ever after.

To Scarlett
with love J.P.

For Mike
with love A.B.

THIS IS A BORZOI BOOK
PUBLISHED BY ALFRED A. KNOPF, INC.

Text copyright © 1991 by Josephine Poole
Illustrations copyright © 1991 by Angela Barrett

All rights reserved under International and Pan-American Copyright Conventions.
Published in the United States by Alfred A. Knopf, Inc., New York. Distributed
by Random House, Inc., New York. Originally published in Great Britain by
Hutchinson Children's Books, an imprint of the Random Century Group Ltd.,
London, in 1991. First American edition, 1992.
Manufactured in Hong Kong 10 9 8 7 6 5 4 3 2 1

Designed by Paul Welti

Library of Congress Cataloging-in-Publication Data
Poole, Josephine.
Snow White / retold by Josephine Poole;
illustrated by Angela Barrett. — 1st American ed.   p.   cm.
"Originally published in Great Britain
by Hutchinson Children's Books…in 1991" — T.p. verso
Summary: A princess takes refuge from her wicked
stepmother in the cottage of seven dwarfs.
ISBN 0-679-82656-4 (trade) — ISBN 0-679-92656-9 (lib. bdg.)
[1. Fairy tales. 2. Folklore—Germany.] I. Barrett, Angela, ill.
II. Schneewittchen. III. Title.
PZ8.P8Sn   1992   398.2—dc20 [E]   91-18411